Snowflakes and Starlight Christmas Poems

Hatty Jones

Published by Hatty Jones, 2024.

This is a work of fiction. Similarities to real people, places, or events are entirely coincidental.

SNOWFLAKES AND STARLIGHT CHRISTMAS POEMS

First edition. November 19, 2024.

Copyright © 2024 Hatty Jones.

ISBN: 979-8230460626

Written by Hatty Jones.

Snowflakes and Starlight Christmas Poems for All Ages

The magic of Christmas is more than the twinkle of lights or the crunch of snow beneath our boots. It's found in the quiet moments—the hush of snowfall, the glow of a candle, the joy of giving, and the wonder in a child's eyes as they gaze at the night sky. It's a season that invites us to pause, reflect, and celebrate what truly matters: love, hope, and the beauty of shared traditions.

Snowflakes and Starlight is a collection of poems crafted for readers young and old, designed to capture the essence of Christmas through the lens of nature's beauty, timeless stories, and heartfelt moments. From the soft descent of snowflakes to the guiding brilliance of starlight, these verses are a reminder of the season's quiet miracles and boundless joys.

Whether you're cozying up by the fire, reading aloud to loved ones, or simply seeking a moment of peace during the holiday rush, this book invites you to step into the magic of Christmas. Each poem is a window into the wonder of the season, reflecting its spirit through themes of togetherness, generosity, and hope.

As you turn these pages, may the poems within bring warmth to your heart, a smile to your face, and the timeless magic of Christmas to your soul. Welcome to Snowflakes and Starlight, where every word is a celebration of the most wonderful time of the year.

Let the journey begin

The First Snowfall

The air turns crisp, a whisper of frost,
A signal that autumn's gold has been lost.
Clouds gather like secrets, heavy and slow,
Bearing the weight of the season's first snow.
The hush of the morning, the stillness profound,
As soft white feathers float to the ground.
Each flake a miracle, fragile and rare,
A fleeting design, spun from winter's care.
Branches wear lacework, delicate and fine,
A fleeting embrace of the cold's design.
Fields and rooftops don robes of white,
Glinting like pearls in the pale morning light.
Children gaze wide-eyed at the magical scene,
Where the earth wears a gown of shimmering sheen.
It stirs up the echoes of days long ago,
When we too danced in the season's first snow.
This gentle arrival, this quiet display,
Transforms the mundane in a magical way.
The first snowfall whispers, a soft winter song,
A promise of beauty to carry us along.

Delicate Grace

The first snow descends with a delicate grace,
Falling like whispers to cover each space.
The world grows softer beneath its touch,
A quieting balm we needed so much.
Each flake a wonder, a crystalline dance,
Catching the light with a glimmering glance.
No two the same, yet together they lay,
Painting the earth in a winter ballet.
Footsteps vanish as quickly as made,
The snow keeps its secrets in shadows and shade.
The chaos is muted, the noise held at bay,
As nature delivers her gift for the day.
The first snow invites us to pause and reflect,
To cherish the silence, the beauty, the effect.
It's a fleeting moment, a gentle debut,
Of winter's arrival, pure and new.

The Artist at Work

Snow falls softly, an artist at work,
Painting the world with a whimsical quirk.
Bare trees now shimmer with crystalline charm,
And the cold bears no hint of menace or harm.
Streetlights glow warmly through curtains of white,
Casting soft halos that pierce the night.
Every step crunches, a satisfying sound,
As winter's first blanket envelops the ground.
The world feels lighter, despite the cold,
A sight worth more than silver or gold.
There's magic in the air, a story untold,
As snowflakes craft memories that never grow old.
A child's laugh echoes, a bell in the frost,
Rekindling joy in hearts long lost.
The first snowfall sings of wonder and cheer,
A promise that magic is always near.

Breath of the Breeze

Snowflakes drift on the breath of the breeze,
Settling gently on branches and leaves.
The world transforms, a canvas of white,
Beneath the soft glow of the pale winter light.
No rush, no hurry; the snow takes its time,
Falling like notes in a wintertime rhyme.
The streets, once grey, are now dressed in grace,
Erasing the past without leaving a trace.
Children burst forth, their laughter a song,
As snowball fights break where silence belongs.
Snow angels form in the soft powder bed,
While dreams of the season swirl in each head.

A Moment so Rare

The first snowfall brings a moment so rare,
A reminder of beauty beyond all compare.
It speaks without words, a gentle refrain,
That even in winter, joy can remain.
The flakes fall soft, a whisper, a sigh,
As clouds release treasures from high in the sky.
The first snow is magic, a moment of bliss,
A quiet embrace, a delicate kiss.
Fields turn to velvet, rooftops to lace,
The world grows gentler, a softer place.
Even the air seems to carry a glow,
Illuminating hearts as it starts to snow.
The first snowfall holds a timeless charm,
A pause in the world, serene and calm.
It carries with it a nostalgic hue,
A bridge between old days and something new.
Children rush out, their mittens held tight,
As snowflakes twirl under soft starlight.
The first snow arrives, a promise, a song,
That winter's magic will carry us along.

The Gathering of Stars

The stars awaken in velvet skies,
Their golden glow begins to rise.
Whispering secrets from far and near,
They sense the magic drawing near.
Like dancers poised in a grand ballet,
They gather close for a wondrous display.
Each star a note in the cosmos' tune,
Guided gently by the crescent moon.
The night is hushed, the world held still,
As starlight glows on the frosted hill.
They shimmer, they sparkle, a celestial choir,
Kindling the heavens with radiant fire.
For Christmas Eve, their brightest show,
A gift for the world, a tender glow.
The stars converge to light the way,
Heralding joy for Christmas Day.

A Starry Symphony

The night hums softly, the stars take their place,
Scattering light in infinite space.
A symphony forms as their light starts to blend,
A cosmic tune that will never end.
The brightest among them leads the song,
Guiding the way for travellers long.
A melody sung in silence and beams,
Filling the night with celestial dreams.
On this sacred eve, their radiance grows,
Shining above the world's quiet snows.
Each glittering star plays a part in the tale,
Of hope that endures when all else may fail.
Their music resounds, though no sound is heard,
A hymn of the heavens, a whispered word.
Starlight on Christmas, a luminous art,
Sings joy to the world, and peace to the heart.

A Star's Christmas Gift

High in the heavens, a star stands alone,
Its glow more radiant than ever known.
It trembles with purpose, its heart alight,
A gift for the world on this holy night.
It calls to its kin with a shimmering cry,
And they gather close in the midnight sky.
A celestial meeting, their mission clear,
To shine their brightest for all to cheer.
Their beams unite in a heavenly thread,
A tapestry woven where angels tread.
Over hills and valleys, their light extends,
A message of love the universe sends.
The stars' gift glows for all to perceive,
On this special night, Christmas Eve.
With every flicker, their story is told,
Of joy unmeasured, and peace untold.

The Celestial Celebration

The stars awaken, their dance begins,
Spinning through skies where silence wins.
A celebration above the earth,
Marking the night of the Savior's birth.
They twinkle and sparkle, a radiant show,
Casting their light on the world below.
The moon joins in with a luminous grin,
Illuminating the wonders within.
From horizon to horizon, the heavens alight,
A festival born on Christmas night.
Each star rejoices in its celestial role,
Weaving together the universe's soul.
Their joy spills over, a shimmering stream,
Filling the night with a radiant dream.
Christmas Eve glows with their festive cheer,
Guiding hearts through the darkest year.

Starry Lanterns of Hope

Lanterns of starlight illuminate the skies,
A beacon of hope as the dark night flies.
They whisper together, a luminous throng,
Their glow a reminder that we all belong.
Each star shines brighter, its purpose clear,
To guide the lost and draw them near.
Their radiance speaks in a gentle plea,
"Come find the love beneath the tree."
The world gazes upward, hearts filled with wonder,
At the luminous art the stars pull asunder.
They light the way for peace to thrive,
Reminding all of the gifts alive.
Starlight on Christmas, a promise above,
To fill the earth with joy and love.
A quiet vigil that carries the year,
Through shadow and sorrow, they reappear.

The Star Path

A path of stars unfurls on high,
Guiding wise travellers through the sky.
Their shimmering lights, a heavenly stream,
Glowing softly like a golden dream.
The trail they weave connects the divine,
Drawing a map with a radiant line.
Over mountains and deserts, it softly flows,
Until it rests where a miracle glows.
Each step they illuminate, steady and true,
Pointing to wonders fresh and new.
For Christmas Eve, they blaze their trail,
A promise of love that will never fail.
Beneath their light, the world finds peace,
A silent moment where worries cease.
The star path shines for those who believe,
A gift of hope on Christmas Eve.

The Star Shepherds

The stars gather like shepherds above,
Tending the sky with their radiant love.
Each one a guide, a sentinel bright,
Guarding the earth through the quiet night.
They whisper secrets of ages past,
Of promises made that forever last.
Their soft glows blend in a sacred hymn,
A luminous prayer sung for Him.
The shepherds of light watch over all,
From icy peaks to the humblest hall.
They lead the weary, the lost, the meek,
To a place where love is all they seek.
On Christmas Eve, their vigil remains,
Through the silent skies and frost-touched plains.
The stars keep watch, steadfast and true,
Guiding the world to something new.

The Starlit Promise

The stars burn brighter on Christmas Eve,
Their glow a promise for hearts to believe.
In their quiet light, the world can see,
A reflection of love's eternity.
Their beams stretch far, crossing all lands,
Reaching out gently like comforting hands.
They touch the hearts of those who despair,
Filling the night with a love so rare.
A starlit sky speaks louder than words,
Its beauty unmatched by songs of birds.
Each twinkle a vow, each shimmer a prayer,
To remind us that hope is always there.
The starlit promise, enduring and true,
Gives strength to many, and light to the few.
On Christmas Eve, their story is clear,
A gift for all, year after year.

Messengers from the Clouds

Born in the clouds, they gather with care,
Crystals of wonder, spun in the air.
Each flake a messenger, delicate and light,
Drifting down softly, a gift of the night.
They spiral and twirl, their journey begins,
Whispering secrets as winter wins.
A blessing they carry, unseen, untold,
Wrapped in their shimmer of silver and gold.
From sky to earth, their dance is serene,
Transforming the world into a glistening scene.
They kiss the ground, a fleeting embrace,
Leaving behind their crystalline trace.
Messengers from above, silent and true,
Bringing the magic of winter to you.

The Flight of the Frozen Stars

Snowflakes shimmer like stars in flight,
Descending softly through the night.
Their journey is swift, yet gentle and calm,
As if carried by nature's tender psalm.
Each flake is a marvel, an icy gem,
A fleeting miracle from nature's hem.
They leap and spin in the chilly breeze,
Dancing lightly among the trees.
Through city streets and forest glades,
They weave their paths in delicate cascades.
Each one unique, yet part of the whole,
A frozen fragment of winter's soul.
The frozen stars touch earth with grace,
Brightening the world in their brief embrace.

Silent Travelers

From clouds above, they leap with glee,
Drifting down to the waiting sea.
Each snowflake whispers a quiet word,
A voice so soft, it's barely heard.
They journey far, across the skies,
Touching the earth as the old year dies.
Each one a traveller, small and light,
Bringing the magic of winter's night.
Through frosty winds, they gently fall,
Blanketing rooftops, meadows, and all.
They vanish quickly, a fleeting sight,
Yet their touch leaves the world alight.
Silent travellers, they come and go,
Leaving behind a world of snow.

Winter's Tiny Carriers

Tiny carriers of winter's cheer,
Snowflakes descend as the cold draws near.
They weave through the air with elegant grace,
Spreading beauty in every place.
Each one crafted with care unseen,
An icy jewel with a frosty sheen.
They glide and twirl, defying time,
As if dancing to nature's rhyme.
Their blessings lie in their quiet fall,
A gentle gift for one and all.
On branches they perch, on cheeks they land,
A fleeting touch of winter's hand.
Carriers of wonder, brief and small,
Yet their beauty enchants us all.

Crystals of Wonder

Crystals of wonder, shaped with intent,
On their journey from the heavens sent.
Spun in silence, kissed by air,
Each one unique, beyond compare.
Through moonlit skies, they softly drift,
A delicate and enchanting gift.
Their spirals dance in the frosty breeze,
Resting gently on rooftops and trees.
With every landing, they bless the ground,
A fleeting miracle, quiet and profound.
Though they vanish beneath the sun's embrace,
Their beauty lingers in every space.
Crystals of wonder, fleeting and bright,
Symbols of joy on a winter's night.

Snowflakes' Whimsical Waltz

Spiralling down in a whimsical waltz,
Snowflakes tumble in dreamy vaults.
Born in the clouds, with intricate care,
They float through the chill of the winter air.
A breeze lifts them high, then lets them fall,
To rest on branches, rooftops, and all.
Their patterns gleam in the faint moonlight,
A fleeting art in the depths of night.
No two alike, they charm the land,
Crafted by nature's unseen hand.
Each one a blessing, a quiet refrain,
Of winter's arrival across the plain.
Snowflakes waltz, a fleeting show,
Adorning the earth with their frosty glow.

The Secret Carriage of Snow

Snowflakes ride on the northern breeze,
Carrying whispers through the trees.
Each one a vessel, secret and small,
Bringing the season's magic to all.
From the heights of clouds, their journey starts,
Bearing the blessings of winter's hearts.
They glide in silence, no need for sound,
Gently blanketing the frozen ground.
Through meadows they drift, to valleys below,
Wrapping the world in a blanket of snow.
Though fleeting, their gift is pure and bright,
A touch of wonder on a frosty night.
The secret carriage moves unseen,
Turning the world to a sparkling scene.

The Snowflakes' Tale

Each snowflake whispers a tale of old,
Spun in the air, fragile and cold.
Their story begins in clouds above,
A journey of beauty, a gift of love.
They drift through the night, soft and slow,
Turning the world to a canvas of snow.
Their tales entwine in the winter breeze,
Carving their mark on branches and eaves.
With every flake, a new story unfolds,
Of distant lands and the cold it holds.
Though their touch is brief, their tales remain,
Carried in hearts like a sweet refrain.
Snowflakes' tales are fleeting, yet true,
A quiet message from sky to you.

Dancers in the Chill

Snowflakes dance in the icy air,
A ballet of beauty, light as a prayer.
Spinning and twirling, they fill the night,
A shimmering vision of frosty delight.
Their journey unfolds in a graceful sweep,
From cloud to ground, where shadows sleep.
Each flake a dancer, unique and free,
Their steps choreographed by winter's decree.
They gather in silence, no sound they bring,
Yet their presence makes the season sing.
On windows they land, on fields they rest,
Each flake performing its radiant best.
Dancers in the chill, brief but divine,
Leaving behind their sparkling design.

The Snowflakes' Blessing

The snowflakes descend, serene and light,
A blessing carried on wings of white.
Born in the heavens, where angels play,
They journey downward, marking their way.
Their touch is gentle, their purpose clear,
To bring winter's magic to all who are near.
Each flake carries a dream, a silent prayer,
A reminder of beauty in the frosty air.
They drift to rest on earth below,
Transforming the mundane to a glittering show.
A fleeting presence, they vanish at dawn,
Yet their message of wonder forever lives on.
The snowflakes' blessing, pure and sweet,
Brings winter's joy to all it meets.

Guardians of the Silent Woods

In the heart of the forest, they quietly stand,
Evergreen sentinels, noble and grand.
Through winter's chill and summer's breeze,
They guard the secrets of whispering trees.
Their branches hold stories of snowflakes and sun,
Of creatures that gather when daylight is done.
They sway with the wind, a silent choir,
Their needles glowing with emerald fire.
When Christmas approaches, they come alive,
Their quiet magic begins to thrive.
Adorned with lights that shimmer and gleam,
They sparkle like stars in a yuletide dream.
The whisper of evergreens carries the song,
Of peace to the world, where hearts belong.
They hold in their arms the essence of cheer,
Standing as symbols of love each year.

The Heartbeat of the Forest

Deep in the forest, where shadows reside,
The evergreen trees in silence abide.
Their whispers are soft, like a tender breeze,
A quiet heartbeat among the trees.
Through winter's frost, they never fade,
A steadfast green in the forest's glade.
Their roots run deep, their arms stretch wide,
A sheltering embrace where secrets hide.
When brought to homes, their voices ring,
Adorned with treasures, they softly sing.
Their needles gleam with the season's light,
A beacon of hope in the dark of night.
They speak of love, of joy reborn,
Of light that pierces the coldest morn.
The whisper of evergreens, ancient and wise,
Guides our hearts beneath winter skies.

The Evergreen's Promise

Amidst the snow and icy breeze,
Stand the steadfast evergreen trees.
Through winter's trials, they proudly bear,
A message of hope in the frosty air.
They whisper softly, their voices low,
Of seasons past and the life they know.
Each needle holds a timeless grace,
A promise that life will never erase.
When decorated with love and care,
They glow with warmth beyond compare.
Their branches cradle ornaments bright,
Reflecting the joy of Christmas night.
The promise they hold is gentle yet clear,
A symbol of life through each passing year.
The evergreen whispers, steady and true,
A beacon of hope for me and you.

The Secrets They Keep

The evergreen trees, so stately and tall,
Hold the secrets of seasons, the wisdom of all.
They whisper of winds, of moonlit skies,
Of fleeting snowflakes and fireflies.
Their roots intertwine in the earth so deep,
Guarding the tales the forest keeps.
Each needle tells of a time long past,
When the world was wild and shadows cast.
When Christmas nears, their silence breaks,
As homes embrace the joy they wake.
Decked with lights and ribbons of gold,
Their ancient magic begins to unfold.
The whispers they share, so soft and light,
Fill the air on a winter's night.
Evergreens murmur, a song of the earth,
Of timeless beauty and endless worth.

The Evergreen's Song

The evergreen trees sing a song of peace,
A melody soft that never will cease.
Through seasons that change and winds that blow,
They stand unyielding in frost and snow.
Their whispers rise with the winter air,
A hymn of resilience, beyond compare.
They cradle the birds, the frost, the light,
A quiet chorus in the velvet night.
When Christmas comes, their voices swell,
Their stories of hope they softly tell.
Adorned with lights, their needles gleam,
A living part of a holiday dream.
Their song is simple, but deep and true,
A message of love for me and you.
The evergreen whispers, eternal and free,
A gift of the forest, an ancient decree.

The Breath of the Evergreens

In the still of the forest, where shadows lie,
The evergreen trees breathe a gentle sigh.
Their needles quiver, their branches sway,
Carrying whispers through night and day.
Their breath is calm, their voices old,
A tale of endurance through frost and cold.
Their roots embrace the frozen ground,
As their whispers rise, a soothing sound.
When Christmas nears, their whispers grow,
Bringing a joy that the heart will know.
Their breath becomes a song so sweet,
A hymn of love the world repeats.
In homes they stand, aglow with cheer,
A symbol of hope through the passing year.
The breath of evergreens, quiet and wise,
Lifts our spirits beneath winter skies.

The Soul of the Forest

Evergreens stand with a quiet grace,
Holding the forest within their embrace.
Their needles shimmer with winter's glow,
The soul of the woods, they softly show.
They whisper of life through frost and shade,
Of creatures that dance in their forest glade.
Their branches reach to the heavens above,
A symbol of strength, resilience, and love.
When dressed in lights, they shine so bright,
Filling the air with Christmas delight.
Their ornaments glint, their tinsel sways,
A celebration of love in the holidays.
Their whispers remind us of timeless things,
Of joy that each Christmas morning brings.
The evergreen trees, serene and strong,
Sing the soul of the forest all winter long.

The Evergreen's Glow

Beneath the stars, the evergreens rest,
Their boughs a haven, their beauty confessed.
Through snow and wind, they hold their ground,
A quiet presence, profound and sound.
Their whispers tell of a world at peace,
Of love that grows, of fears that cease.
Their needles glisten with morning frost,
A reminder of life that's never lost.
When lights adorn their sturdy arms,
They radiate warmth with timeless charms.
Their glow reflects a season of cheer,
Bringing us hope year after year.
The evergreen trees, in moonlight's glow,
Carry the joy that we long to know.
Their whispers linger, soft and true,
A promise of light for me and you.

The Trees That Never Sleep

Through endless winters, the evergreens stay,
Their needles sharp in the soft light of day.
They whisper of seasons that come and go,
Of blankets of ice and rivers that flow.
Their stillness hides a heart alive,
A quiet strength through which they thrive.
Though snow may weigh their branches low,
Their spirit endures beneath the glow.
On Christmas Eve, they softly gleam,
A part of every holiday dream.
Decked with ornaments, ribbons, and light,
They guard the magic of Christmas night.
The trees that never sleep remain,
A beacon of hope through joy and pain.
Their whispers rise, serene and deep,
A song of love they always keep.

The Evergreen's Embrace

The evergreen trees stand tall and strong,
Holding the world in their arms all along.
Their branches extend, a loving reach,
A silent sermon that nature will teach.
Through snow and frost, they softly hum,
A melody sweet as winter's drum.
Their whispers comfort, their presence calms,
A soothing touch in the forest's palms.
Dressed in ornaments, sparkling and bright,
They come alive in the Christmas light.
Their needles gleam with a frosty cheer,
A glowing beacon of love and fear.
The evergreen trees embrace us all,
Standing steadfast through winter's call.
Their whispers remind us to hold love near,
In the magic of Christmas, year after year.

The Silver Sleigh's Flight

Under the moon's soft, silvery glow,
A sleigh waits atop a blanket of snow.
Its runners glint, its reins are tight,
Ready to soar through the starry night.
I climb aboard, my heart takes flight,
As the horses leap into endless light.
The winds sing songs of frosty cheer,
Whispering tales for only me to hear.
Through crystal skies and twinkling stars,
We journey past galaxies, near and far.
Auroras ripple in radiant streams,
A dream unfolding in shimmering beams.
Myths come alive as we glide with grace,
Sprites and elves with glowing face.
The midnight sleigh carries me far,
To a world untouched, where wonders are.

A Journey Beneath the Stars

The sleigh is light, the reins are gold,
Its frame a relic of stories old.
With a jingle of bells, we rise in the air,
Bound for a world beyond compare.
The stars wink down, their light so near,
A cosmic path through skies so clear.
The moon smiles wide, her beams aglow,
Guiding us over the hills below.
Frosted forests and icy streams,
Pass beneath us like fleeting dreams.
A herd of reindeer gallops high,
Their laughter echoing in the sky.
We chase the comet's fiery tail,
Through velvet night on a wondrous trail.
The sleigh ride ends as dawn appears,
But its magic lingers for endless years.

The Enchanted Sleigh

The sleigh appeared from a winter mist,
Its frame adorned with an icy twist.
The reins were held by hands unseen,
A driver cloaked in a moonbeam sheen.
"Come, ride with me," the figure said,
As stars above shone bright and red.
With a leap of faith, I took my place,
And off we soared through time and space.
The winds carried us over frozen seas,
Through forests alive with singing trees.
A polar bear waved from an icy shore,
While snowflakes danced in a soft downpour.
We met the aurora, its colors untamed,
It whispered secrets that cannot be named.
The sleigh then landed in a world so bright,
Where dreams awaken in the Christmas night.

The Starry Path

The sleigh awaits in a field of white,
Its runners gleaming in the pale moonlight.
With a crack of the whip, the steeds take flight,
And I'm swept away through the endless night.
We follow a trail of sparkling stars,
Past glowing planets and frozen bars.
The Milky Way spills its golden streams,
As we journey deeper into dreams.
A snowman waves from a distant hill,
While frost sprites twirl with dainty skill.
An ice dragon roars, its breath so cold,
A guardian of treasures and stories untold.
The sleigh keeps flying, my heart beats fast,
Through a magical world that will ever last.
The path of stars shines bold and bright,
Leading me home through the Christmas night.

The Moonlit Sleigh

Under the moon's serene embrace,
The sleigh awaits in a shadowed place.
Its bells ring softly, their tune a call,
To venture beyond the world we know at all.
With a leap of courage, I take my seat,
As the horses gallop on nimble feet.
Through frosted clouds and starry skies,
The sleigh ascends where no bird flies.
We glide past mountains cloaked in snow,
Where ancient secrets slumber below.
Elves and goblins wave from afar,
As we dance in the light of a shooting star.
The moon hums low, her song a guide,
Through the endless night on this magical ride.
And as the sleigh lands with morning near,
The memory shines, forever clear.

Sleigh Bells and Stardust

The sleigh was crafted from silver and dreams,
Its runners carved from moonlit beams.
The bells on its reins sang a magical tune,
As it soared through the skies of Christmas June.
We raced with comets, their tails ablaze,
Through nebula clouds and astral haze.
Each turn revealed a new delight,
In this wondrous realm of eternal night.
A phoenix soared in fiery display,
Its feathers alight with the coming day.
Sprites of frost danced on the sleigh,
Their laughter echoing as we sped away.
The stardust clung to my face and hair,
A token of magic beyond compare.
And though the ride ended at dawn's first ray,
Its starlit magic will forever stay.

The Sleigh of Dreams

A sleigh of gold with reins of fire,
Promised a journey to lift me higher.
Its driver smiled with eyes so wise,
And pointed us toward the endless skies.
We soared above the winter land,
Through auroras painted by heaven's hand.
The stars grew close, their warmth I felt,
As cosmic wonders around me dwelt.
We met the North Wind, fierce and bold,
His icy breath a story told.
Below, the earth was calm and still,
Its snow-clad valleys and frosted hills.
The sleigh whispered secrets as we raced on,
Of dreams unspoken and nights long gone.
It carried me home through the endless blue,
Leaving my heart both full and new.

Riders of the Midnight Sky

In the midnight sky, where silence lies,
A sleigh ascends, its reins untied.
The wind's embrace pulls us higher still,
Over frozen rivers and winter's chill.
The stars above are close enough to touch,
Their glittering lights a radiant clutch.
Comets streak past with fiery trails,
As we ride through the night's ancient tales.
Below, the wolves sing their mournful tune,
Howling low at the silver moon.
Above, the heavens stretch wide and vast,
A realm of beauty, free from the past.
The sleigh dives low, then soars anew,
A timeless dance through the icy blue.
And as we return to the earth below,
The midnight sky keeps its gentle glow.

A Sleigh Ride Through Legends

The sleigh moves swift through frosted air,
Carrying dreams and magic rare.
Each jingle of bells echoes the past,
Of ancient legends that forever last.
We meet a frost giant on a snowy peak,
His icy laughter both cold and bleak.
A fleet of swans with wings of gold,
Guide us through myths untold.
The Northern Lights shimmer and sway,
Lighting our path on this magical day.
The sleigh glides through time's open door,
To lands of wonder, tales, and lore.
The legends whisper as we fly by,
Of heroes, dreams, and a starry sky.
And though the ride ends as dawn appears,
The myths we touched linger through the years.

Through the Veil of Winter's Night

The sleigh cuts through the winter's veil,
On a journey rare, an enchanted tale.
The horses gallop, their manes alight,
Pulling us higher into the night.
A crystal palace stands far below,
Its towers gleaming with icy glow.
Fairies flit in their frosted gowns,
Dancing circles on snowy crowns.
Above, the stars hum their gentle tune,
Guiding our sleigh by the light of the moon.
We pass through clouds of sparkling frost,
Into a realm where time is lost.
The veil parts wide as we race on through,
Revealing wonders both old and new.
The sleigh descends as the journey ends,
But its magic lives where the heart pretends.

Beacon of Hope

A single candle flickers in the night,
A fragile flame, yet burning bright.
Its glow is soft, a golden hue,
A promise made for hearts to renew.
Through frosted glass, its light is seen,
A steadfast warmth, calm and serene.
It whispers softly to those who roam,
"Come find your shelter, come find your home."
The wind may howl, the snow may fall,
But this small light outshines it all.
A beacon of hope, it gently gleams,
Guiding the lost to their cherished dreams.
A candle in the window, pure and true,
Holds the promise of love, for me and you.

The Window's Flame

Upon the sill, the candle stands,
Its glow as warm as gentle hands.
It lights the way for those afar,
A guiding flame, a humble star.
Through icy winds and winter's chill,
Its steadfast flame refuses to still.
It calls to hearts both near and far,
"Come rest your soul, wherever you are."
The window glows, the frost recedes,
Its warmth fulfils the spirit's needs.
A simple flame, yet it contains,
The power to soothe all earthly pains.
A candle burns, its light remains,
A timeless glow through nights and rains.

The Flame of Welcome

The candle burns, a quiet glow,
Through the pane where frost may grow.
Its warmth reaches out, a silent plea,
For wanderers lost on a restless sea.
Its flicker tells of love inside,
Of doors flung wide and arms opened wide.
Through storm and snow, it lights the way,
To welcome the weary at the end of day.
A flame of welcome, humble and true,
It speaks without words to both me and you.
It whispers of hearth, of stories to share,
Of kindness and warmth beyond compare.
A single candle, soft and bright,
Shines out with love through the coldest night.

Guardian of the Dark

In the darkest hour, the candle stands,
A fragile flame in steadfast hands.
It guards the night, it keeps the watch,
A tiny sun on a frost-kissed porch.
Its glow repels the creeping cold,
Its story ancient, yet never old.
It hums a song of love's embrace,
A radiant warmth in the loneliest space.
The shadows stretch, the winds may cry,
Yet still it burns, a star close by.
It guards the hearts of those inside,
And welcomes travellers, arms open wide.
A guardian flame, both strong and slight,
A symbol of hope through the endless night.

A Silent Flame

The candle's flame is soft and small,
Yet holds a strength that outshines all.
It whispers gently through the pane,
A tale of hope through joy and pain.
Its light defies the winter's chill,
A steady glow that warms and stills.
It speaks to hearts in shadows cast,
Of brighter days and struggles past.
The snow may fall, the winds may moan,
But this small flame stands all alone.
Its silence comforts, its light reveals,
The love that every home conceals.
A candle glows, its meaning clear,
A silent prayer for those held dear.

The Candle's Watch

Through the storm, the candle glows,
Its warmth a balm for weary souls.
Its light is steady, soft, and low,
A promise made to those who know.
It keeps its watch through darkest night,
A symbol pure, a guiding light.
Its flicker whispers, "Come this way,
Find peace and rest, if just today."
The frost may gather, the winds may roar,
But still it shines, a silent core.
The candle stands, unbowed, unseen,
A sentinel bright where shadows lean.
In every heart, its flame is kept,
A spark of hope that's softly wept.

The Candle's Glow

The candle burns, its glow divine,
A quiet voice through space and time.
It reaches out through snow and frost,
To guide the lonely who feel lost.
Its light is simple, pure, and clear,
A call to love, a call to near.
Through winter's bite, its warmth remains,
A golden balm for icy pains.
In every flicker, there's a prayer,
For peace and love to fill the air.
Its glow reflects the heart's true plea,
For joy and warmth in unity.
The candle's glow, so small yet vast,
Connects the present with the past.

A Light Through the Cold

Through frosty panes, the candle gleams,
A guiding light for wandering dreams.
Its glow cuts through the darkest frost,
A beacon for those who've felt lost.
Its flame is steady, its warmth so near,
A silent song for those who hear.
It speaks of home, of fires aglow,
Of hands held tight through ice and snow.
Though storms may rage and tempests rise,
This candle shines through blackened skies.
Its purpose clear, its mission plain,
To offer solace through cold and pain.
A single flame, a promise shown,
No one is ever truly alone.

A Light Eternal

The candle flickers, its warmth alive,
Through winter's chill, it seems to thrive.
It beckons softly to those who roam,
To find their place, to come back home.
Its flame is small, yet mighty still,
It warms the heart, it bends the will.
Through icy gusts, its light holds true,
A steadfast glow for me and you.
No matter how cold the night may be,
Its flicker shines for all to see.
Its meaning clear, its presence kind,
A flame that guards both heart and mind.
A light eternal, soft yet bright,
The candle burns through every night.

A Flame for the Soul

The candle burns in its quiet grace,
A glow of peace in a shadowed space.
Its light reflects on frosted glass,
A flame of love that will not pass.
Its whispers soothe, its warmth conveys,
A silent hymn for winter's days.
Through storm and snow, it holds its place,
A tiny star in a vast, cold space.
It welcomes all who see its glow,
A sign of love the heart will know.
Its light a promise, pure and true,
Of hope reborn for me and you.
A flame for the soul, a steady guide,
A candle shines through the night outside.

The Stillness of the Snow

The sleigh comes to rest, the reindeer pause,
Their breath in clouds like nature's applause.
Santa steps down, his boots in the snow,
To marvel at the world in its midnight glow.
The chimneys can wait, the gifts will remain,
For this quiet moment, he takes the reign.
The stars above, the moon so bright,
The peaceful hush of a Christmas night.
No child stirs, no sound disturbs,
Just the rustling trees and the call of birds.
Santa smiles, his heart aglow,
At the simple beauty the world can show.
In the stillness, he finds a gift so rare,
A quiet peace that hangs in the air.
For even Santa, busy and kind,
Needs the magic of stillness to clear his mind.

A Pause Beneath the Stars

Amid the bustle of his yearly flight,
Santa pauses to admire the night.
The sleigh is grounded, the reindeer graze,
Under the sky's celestial haze.
The snow reflects the starry gleam,
A glittering world that feels like a dream.
The wind whispers through the frosted trees,
A lullaby carried on winter's breeze.
Santa sighs, his breath a mist,
Grateful for the moment he almost missed.
The beauty of Christmas, calm and serene,
The quiet joy of the evergreen.
For one small moment, the world stands still,
And Santa feels his heart refill.
A pause beneath the starlit dome,
Before the journey brings him home.

The Silent Watcher

Santa stands where the snow lies deep,
The world around him fast asleep.
His sack of gifts rests by the sleigh,
As he watches the world in soft array.
The moonlight paints the snow in gold,
A sight more precious than gifts untold.
The silence hums with an ancient tune,
The quiet magic of Christmas's moon.
A fox darts past, its coat aglow,
A shadow blending with the snow.
Santa smiles, his heart at peace,
In this moment, all worries cease.
The silent world, so calm and bright,
Fills him with awe on this sacred night.
Santa the giver, now the receiver,
Of nature's gift, the quiet believer.

The Frost-Kissed Pause

Santa halts his midnight ride,
And lets the world in silence abide.
The sleigh sits still, its bells at rest,
While snowflakes fall, a silken crest.
The earth is wrapped in a frosty cloak,
A peaceful charm that's softly spoke.
The stars above, a guiding choir,
Sparkle like embers in a celestial fire.
The reindeer snuffle, their breath in the air,
While Santa marvels at a world so rare.
The rush of the night, the lists, the toys,
Fade to the background of simple joys.
He treasures the stillness, the perfect sight,
Of Christmas Eve bathed in tranquil light.
For even Santa, with duties unending,
Finds peace in the beauty the night is lending.

A Moment to Reflect

Santa pauses, his work half-done,
Under the gaze of the midnight sun.
The North Wind carries a tune so low,
Through shimmering trees and fields of snow.
He gazes out at the frozen streams,
Lost for a moment in quiet dreams.
The world seems softer, gentler now,
A gift he cherishes, though he knows not how.
The stars above seem closer tonight,
Their glow a balm, their peace a light.
Even the sleigh, so ready to fly,
Waits for Santa beneath the sky.
In this quiet moment, his heart is full,
The beauty of Christmas, eternal and cool.
And as he resumes his magical quest,
He carries with him this moment of rest.

A Winter's Reverie

Santa steps from his sleigh to the snow,
And breathes the crisp air, soft and slow.
The bustle of work, the hum of the sleigh,
Fade for a moment in winter's display.
The snow glitters like a sea of stars,
Under the gaze of Venus and Mars.
The forest hums with a muted cheer,
A sound so faint it's hard to hear.
He leans on his sleigh, his eyes alight,
At the quiet beauty of Christmas night.
A simple peace, a world aglow,
A gift only Santa could truly know.
He lingers a while, his heart at ease,
With the song of the wind through the ancient trees.
Then with a smile, he takes the reins,
Refreshed by the night's enchanting refrain.

The Night's Gift

On a hilltop draped in a snowy sheet,
Santa halts for a quiet retreat.
His boots sink deep, his breath is slow,
As he marvels at the world below.
The village sleeps, its lights agleam,
A picture perfect as a dream.
The moon above, a watchful guide,
Casts silver beams on the countryside.
The reindeer rest, their heads held low,
As Santa Savors the peace of snow.
The stars seem brighter, the air so clear,
A moment of joy that draws him near.
For this is the gift the night can bring,
A pause for the soul, a moment to sing.
Santa smiles, his spirit alight,
Grateful for the beauty of this quiet night.

A Glimpse of Peace

Santa halts his busy ride,
And steps into the world outside.
The wind is cold, the snow is deep,
The earth itself seems fast asleep.
Yet in the stillness, life remains,
The rustling trees, the frozen plains.
A hare leaps softly across the field,
Its presence quiet, its joy concealed.
The stars above seem close, so near,
Their radiance clear, their message dear.
Santa gazes, his heart made light,
By the tranquil beauty of this sacred night.
For even he, with tasks unending,
Finds peace in the quiet the night is lending.
And as he resumes his heavenly flight,
He carries the stillness of Christmas night.

The Snow-Covered World

Santa's sleigh rests by an open glade,
Where moonlight dances and shadows fade.
He steps to the earth, his boots sink low,
Into the hush of the purest snow.
The world is soft, its edges blurred,
As if time itself has been deterred.
The trees bow low beneath their frost,
A quiet wonder at no cost.
The stars seem brighter, the air so still,
As Santa drinks his heart's fill.
This snow-covered world, a treasure untold,
Glows in the night, both bright and cold.
Santa's eyes glimmer, his smile wide,
As he takes in the peace of the countryside.
And though his journey must soon resume,
This moment of calm clears all gloom.

The Magic of the Quiet Night

Santa halts his sleigh mid-flight,
To admire the world bathed in moonlight.
The reindeer pause, their breaths like steam,
While Santa steps into a quiet dream.
The snow-covered hills gleam soft and white,
A magical world in the still of night.
The forest whispers, the stars hum low,
As the frosted air begins to glow.
A fox slips by, its coat a flame,
A fleeting glimpse of nature's claim.
Santa smiles, his heart aglow,
At the wondrous beauty of the snow.
For even he, with gifts to share,
Finds time to pause and simply care.
In the magic of the quiet night,
Santa finds his own delight.

Winter's Symphony

The North Wind rises, its voice a song,
A melody ancient, fierce, and strong.
It sweeps through trees with a whistling cry,
A symphony born where clouds meet sky.
The branches sway to its rhythmic beat,
A dance of nature, wild yet sweet.
It hums through valleys, a haunting refrain,
Echoing softly in the frosty plain.
The snowflakes twirl to its airy tune,
Beneath the gaze of the pale, full moon.
Icicles chime as its fingers pass,
A tinkling bell from the winter's glass.
The North Wind's music fills the night,
A carol of frost, serene and bright.
Its song is timeless, a gift it brings,
A wintry hymn that the whole world sings.

The Wind's Frosty Choir

The North Wind calls with a chilling note,
Through icy meadows its whispers float.
It sings to the stars, it hums to the trees,
A frosty anthem that rides the breeze.
The rivers freeze to its steady song,
While echoes ripple the land along.
Each gust a verse, each breeze a line,
A carol composed in winter's design.
It whistles through chimneys, it howls through the night,
A sound both eerie and full of delight.
Its tune is sharp, yet strangely kind,
A melody carved from the coldest wind.
The North Wind's choir swells and soars,
A hymn that drifts through winter's doors.
Its voice is nature's, fierce and free,
Singing the heart of eternity.

The North Wind's Lullaby

The North Wind whispers, its voice so low,
A lullaby soft through the falling snow.
It cradles the world in its frozen arms,
A tune of winter's quiet charms.
Its breath is icy, its touch is light,
Yet its song warms the coldest night.
Through shadowed woods and fields aglow,
It carries the dreams of all below.
It croons to the moon, it sighs to the sea,
A tender refrain of serenity.
The stars join in with their twinkling cheer,
Their silent notes echoing near.
The North Wind's song is a soothing balm,
A winter's lullaby, peaceful and calm.
Its melody lingers in every ear,
Filling the world with holiday cheer.

The Whispering Wind

The North Wind whispers a quiet tune,
Through snowy forests beneath the moon.
It stirs the branches, it sweeps the plains,
A haunting melody in frosty veins.
The trees respond with a gentle creak,
Their voices blending in whispers meek.
The snow replies with a soft, crisp crunch,
A harmony born with each icy punch.
It drifts through chimneys, it taps on doors,
It races across the frozen shores.
Its rhythm dances in whirls of white,
A fleeting song in the depth of night.
The North Wind's music, fleeting and true,
Is nature's gift for me and you.
Its carol resounds, its beauty stays,
A wintry hymn for the year's cold days.

Frost's Silent Orchestra

The North Wind gathers an orchestra grand,
Composed of snow, ice, and the land.
Its baton sweeps through frosty air,
Conducting a song beyond compare.
The pine trees hum with rustling leaves,
While frozen rivers add gentle heaves.
The snowflakes swirl in rhythmic delight,
Their silent dance a song of night.
The icicles chime like glassy bells,
Each note a story the winter tells.
The wind takes center stage to sing,
Its voice a symphony echoing.
Together they play a timeless song,
Of winter's beauty, fierce and strong.
The music of frost fills the air,
A masterpiece crafted with tender care.

The Wind's Cold Melody

The North Wind croons with a chilling sound,
A melody sung where snow is found.
It curls through valleys, it skips through hills,
A frosty tune that the night fulfils.
Its notes are sharp, its rhythm bold,
A song of winter, icy and cold.
Yet in its breath lies a gentle grace,
A haunting beauty time won't erase.
The night listens close, the stars lean near,
Drawn by the wind's ethereal cheer.
Its melody climbs through winter's haze,
Filling the dark with its frosted praise.
The North Wind's tune lingers and weaves,
Through bare tree branches and snow-draped eaves.
Its song is fleeting, yet it remains,
A melody etched in icy veins.

The Wind's Frozen Dance

The North Wind dances with icy flair,
Spinning and twirling through frozen air.
Its steps are swift, its movements free,
A swirling waltz of melody.
The snowflakes join, they spin and leap,
In patterns the wind alone can keep.
The trees bow low in a graceful bend,
As the frosty dance refuses to end.
The rhythm quickens, the night grows loud,
As the wind waltzes beneath the cloud.
Its song is wild, its tempo clear,
A hymn to the winter's frosty cheer.
But as dawn breaks and the night retreats,
The dance slows down, the music beats.
The North Wind sighs its final refrain,
Promising to waltz through the night again.

Frost's Ancient Hymn

The North Wind hums an ancient hymn,
Its icy voice both sharp and grim.
It carries the weight of ages past,
Through endless winters, cold and vast.
Its tone is mournful, yet full of light,
A melody sung on the longest night.
The trees bow low, their branches sway,
As the wind's refrain carries them away.
The frost replies with its crackling sound,
A percussive beat on frozen ground.
The stars above lend their silent grace,
To the North Wind's hymn in time and space.
Its song reminds the world below,
That winter's beauty is meant to show.
Though cold and harsh, its music brings,
The quiet joy that the North Wind sings.

The Wind's Frosty Ballad

The North Wind sings a ballad slow,
A tale of frost and drifting snow.
It tells of forests cloaked in white,
And whispers of stars on a winter's night.
Its voice is haunting, filled with grace,
A chilling tune from time and space.
It echoes through the icy plain,
A song of beauty, joy, and pain.
The snowdrifts rise in gentle waves,
Responding to the tune it gave.
The frost etches patterns on windowpanes,
Inspired by the wind's sweet refrains.
The ballad ends as dawn appears,
But lingers in the heart for years.
The North Wind's voice, both sharp and kind,
Leaves its melody in the winter wind.

A Carol of the Chill

The North Wind howls a carol clear,
Its song the anthem of the year.
It rushes high, it dives so low,
A symphony born of ice and snow.
The frost joins in with its crackling tune,
Harmonizing beneath the moon.
The trees respond with creaks and groans,
Adding their depth to the wind's sweet tones.
Each gust a verse, each breeze a rhyme,
A carol sung through frozen time.
Its voice surrounds, its power stays,
A melody for the coldest days.
The North Wind's carol sweeps the land,
A timeless hymn of winter's hand.
Its music lingers, haunting and deep,
A song that sings while the world's asleep.

The True Gift

No ribbon or bow can match the glow,
Of kindness shared where hearts may go.
No paper bright, no fancy string,
Can rival the joy true love will bring.
A gentle word, a helping hand,
A promise made, a heartfelt stand.
These gifts are wrapped in acts so pure,
Their memory lingers, their meaning sure.
A warm embrace when hope feels lost,
A friend who stays despite the cost.
A stranger's smile, a thoughtful deed,
A seed of kindness, a growing creed.
These are the gifts that time won't fade,
No shelf or store where they are made.
They're born in hearts, in love's sweet art,
Wrapped in kindness, soul to heart.

The Gift of Giving

The best gifts aren't found beneath the tree,
But in the love we give for free.
A quiet moment, a listening ear,
A word of comfort when life feels drear.
It's in the laughter shared with friends,
In bonds of love that never end.
A hand that lifts, a heart that stays,
Through trials dark and endless days.
It's not the gift, but how it's given,
A token small, yet love-driven.
A note, a hug, a gentle thought,
A memory formed without being bought.
For kindness is the truest treasure,
A gift beyond all worldly measure.
Wrapped not in paper, but in grace,
A love that time cannot erase.

A Ribbon of Care

The finest gift comes without a bow,
A simple kindness that seeds can grow.
It doesn't shimmer, it doesn't shine,
But it's the most treasured gift of time.
A visit made to an elder's side,
A hand to help through the roughest tide.
A laugh to chase away the rain,
A gentle balm for silent pain.
These gifts of care, these threads of love,
Are blessings sent from realms above.
They weave a fabric strong and true,
A tapestry shared between me and you.
No shop can sell, no price can claim,
A kindness given without aim.
For gifts like these, so rare, so bright,
Are wrapped in care and pure delight.

Wrapped in Thoughtfulness

The gift that lingers through the years,
Is often wrapped in love and tears.
A thoughtful act, a heartfelt word,
A song of kindness softly heard.
It's in the moments we choose to share,
A hand extended, a tender care.
The way we stand when others fall,
The way we answer a desperate call.
A gift of thought can change the day,
It lifts the dark and lights the way.
It doesn't come in a fancy pack,
But in the warmth we give back.
Thoughtfulness is the truest art,
A gift that dwells within the heart.
Wrapped in kindness, tied with grace,
It leaves the world a brighter place.

The Heart's Wrapping

No store can sell the gift of peace,
The joy that comes when worries cease.
It's in the love we freely give,
The way we help each other live.
A child's laughter, a friend's embrace,
A stranger's kindness in a hurried place.
A quiet gesture, a thoughtful deed,
A moment to meet another's need.
The heart wraps gifts no hand can make,
A blessing shared for kindness' sake.
It's not the glitter, nor shiny bows,
But in the love that softly glows.
For gifts of heart need no disguise,
Their beauty shines in grateful eyes.
And though they're small, they carry weight,
The power to heal, to elevate.

Beyond the Wrapping

The gifts that matter leave no trace,
But linger long in time and space.
They're in the kindness freely shown,
The seeds of love the heart has sown.
A call to someone feeling low,
A way to let your caring show.
A meal prepared with quiet thought,
A moment shared, a lesson taught.
These gifts are small, yet deeply felt,
Their impact long, their meaning heartfelt.
No wrapping needed, no glittered hue,
Just simple kindness shining through.
Beyond the paper, beyond the string,
Are gifts that make the spirit sing.
For love and thoughtfulness freely shared,
Are treasures beyond what's ever prepared.

Tied with Compassion

The gifts that shine are often unseen,
Not wrapped in paper, but softly keen.
They're in the way we touch a heart,
In every place where kindness starts.
A tear wiped dry, a soothing word,
A story told, a voice that's heard.
A promise kept when times are tough,
The way we say, "You are enough."
Compassion wraps these gifts of care,
A tender light that's always there.
No bow, no tag, just love displayed,
In every moment kindness is made.
Tied with care, these gifts remain,
A lasting balm for joy and pain.
For in compassion, we always find,
The truest gifts for humankind.

A Touch of Grace

Gifts of grace come soft and light,
A whispered word in the darkest night.
They're in the way we take the time,
To heal a hurt, to share a rhyme.
A letter sent, a warm hello,
A kindness felt when spirits grow low.
A hug that lingers, a shared delight,
A gift of care that feels so right.
No fancy wrap, no glittered gleam,
Just the love that makes a dream.
A touch of grace, a moment shared,
A lasting memory that shows we cared.
For in these gifts, the heart is bare,
Revealing love beyond compare.
Wrapped in kindness, soft and true,
A touch of grace for me and you.

Kindness Unwrapped

The best gifts need no box or bow,
They're found in kindness we always show.
A seat offered, a hand outstretched,
A bond of love that can't be matched.
A smile shared across the way,
A helping hand on a busy day.
A moment paused to ease a fear,
A simple act to bring good cheer.
These gifts, though small, are deeply strong,
They linger near, they last so long.
No glitter, no ribbon, just acts of care,
That show the world we're always there.
For kindness unwrapped is the finest thing,
A gift of the heart that makes it sing.
And though unseen, it always shows,
The love that within the giver flows.

Gifts Without Ribbons

The finest gifts wear no disguise,
They shine through love in grateful eyes.
No ribbons tied, no paper torn,
But acts of kindness gently born.
A door held open, a place to rest,
A smile that lifts a weary chest.
A word of hope, a quiet ear,
A moment shared to draw us near.
These gifts are timeless, always true,
They hold the power to renew.
No price to pay, no box to fill,
Just love and care through thought and will.
For gifts without ribbons mean so much,
They warm the soul with every touch.
And in their giving, the world can see,
The beauty of true humanity.

The Little Star's Dream

High in the sky, a small star shone,
Feeling unseen, and all alone.
The other stars laughed, "You're far too dim,
No one will notice your little hymn."
But deep inside, the star held tight,
A dream to shine with all its might.
One Christmas Eve, a voice rang clear,
"We need your glow to guide us near!"
The little star beamed, its light so bright,
It led the way through the darkest night.
And from that day, the heavens all knew,
The smallest star can have the brightest view.

The Star That Found Its Shine

A little star sat in the velvet sky,
Watching the big ones sparkle high.
"They're brighter than me," the small star sighed,
"I'll never shine like them," it cried.
But on Christmas Eve, the angels came,
Calling the star by its humble name.
"Tonight, we need your special light,
To guide the world through this holy night."
The star glowed bright, its heart aglow,
A light so pure, it set the world aglow.
Now it shines with pride, up above,
A reminder of hope, faith, and love.

The Overlooked Light

A small star blinked in the vast night sky,
Wishing it could soar so high.
It tried to twinkle, it tried to gleam,
But it seemed too faint for the world's big dream.
The brighter stars would laugh and play,
While the little one watched from far away.
But on Christmas night, a child looked up,
And wished for hope from their empty cup.
The little star answered with all its might,
Filling the world with guiding light.
It learned that even the smallest glow,
Can light the path for hearts to know.

The Star's Christmas Night

The little star watched from afar,
Dreaming of being a guiding star.
"I'm not big, and I'm not grand,"
It thought as it twinkled above the land.
But one cold night, so clear and bright,
The little star shone with all its might.
A shepherd looked up, and so did the wise,
Guided by the star through starlit skies.
The little star led them to a place,
Where a miracle lay in a humble space.
Now every Christmas, its story is told,
Of a little star with a heart of gold.

The Brave Little Star

In the sky, a little star hid,
Afraid to shine as the others did.
"I'm not as bold, I'm not as bright,"
It whispered low in the still of night.
But when the angels called for aid,
The little star was not afraid.
It glowed so strong, it led the way,
To where a baby in a manger lay.
Now the little star shines every year,
A beacon of love and Christmas cheer.
Its light reminds us all to see,
The power of faith and humility.

The Forgotten Star

The little star sat in the corner of space,
Watching the others with shining grace.
"They're brighter than me," it softly sighed,
Feeling its light was unjustified.
But on a night so cold and still,
A voice called out with a heavenly will.
"You're perfect for this, your glow so true,
To guide the world to something new."
The little star twinkled with all its might,
Leading the way through the Christmas night.
From that day on, it knew its place,
A star of love, of light, and grace.

The Humble Spark

In the heavens, a star sat small,
Feeling unseen by the great and tall.
It watched the others dazzle and gleam,
And thought, "I'm too faint for anyone's dream."
But the heavens turned on a special night,
When the little star found its light.
It guided the wise, it showed the way,
To where a child in a manger lay.
The little star shone like never before,
A tiny spark that opened a door.
Now it gleams with pride for all to see,
A lesson in faith and humility.

The Star That Believed

A tiny star flickered, hidden and shy,
Watching the world from the vast, dark sky.
"I'm not enough," it often thought,
For the grander stars, it felt it was not.
But one clear night, a miracle came,
And angels called it by its name.
"We need your light, small though you seem,
To guide the way to a newborn dream."
The little star beamed with all its heart,
Illuminating the world with its part.
It learned its size didn't matter at all,
Even the smallest can stand tall.

The Shy Star's Moment

A shy little star stayed out of sight,
Afraid to shine in the cold, dark night.
The others danced and sparkled high,
While it flickered faintly in the sky.
But on Christmas Eve, a call rang out,
"We need your glow, without a doubt!"
The star shone strong, its light so pure,
Leading the world with a heart secure.
It found its place among the great,
A shining guide to heaven's gate.
The shy little star grew bold that night,
A humble hero in the Christmas light.

The Star That Led the Way

In the sky, a star felt small,
Its light so faint, its shine so dull.
"I'll never matter," it often said,
While brighter stars gleamed overhead.
But one still night, a voice it heard,
"You're needed now to spread the word.
Shine your light and guide the way,
To where the miracle child will lay."
The little star twinkled, its heart so true,
And led the wise men to something new.
It learned its light, though small, could gleam,
And guide the world to a Christmas dream.

Dancing in the Snow

The children dash through frosted air,
Laughter ringing everywhere.
They tumble down on blankets white,
And spread their arms with pure delight.
Their hands and feet begin to sway,
Creating wings where snowflakes lay.
Each angel forms beneath their spin,
A magic world where dreams begin.
They gaze above at skies of grey,
Where more soft flakes will join their play.
In snow angels, their joy takes flight,
A masterpiece of purest light.

Wings of Winter

The snow lies soft, a canvas wide,
Where children's dreams can't be denied.
They fall and laugh, their cheeks aglow,
Their giggles lost in fields of snow.
With sweeping arms and kicking feet,
Their snowy angels come complete.
Each form a mark of fleeting fun,
A winter's gift beneath the sun.
The world seems brighter, pure and true,
As angels grow where frost winds blew.
In every sweep, their hearts take wing,
In snowbound joy that dreams can bring.

Frosty Fantasies

The children leap into the frost,
Their world of worries quickly lost.
They lie beneath the cloudy skies,
And spread their arms with sparkling eyes.
With every move, a form takes shape,
An angel born in winter's cape.
Their laughter swirls like the falling snow,
A melody where innocence grows.
The angels rise, a fleeting dream,
Like stars reflected in a stream.
And as they play, the magic stays,
A memory bright for winter days.

Angel Wings Unfurled

The snow invites the children near,
Its chilly touch brings endless cheer.
They fall and sweep with arms out wide,
Their laughter fills the countryside.
Each motion carves a frosty wing,
A winter angel shimmering.
The cold is naught, their hearts are warm,
Creating joy in every form.
Above, the sky is soft and grey,
A perfect dome for their display.
And when they rise, the angels stay,
A testament to their bright play.

Whispers in the Snow

The snowflakes fall like whispered dreams,
In sparkling white and moonlit beams.
The children tumble, their giggles soar,
As angels bloom on the frosty floor.
With arms outstretched, they paint the snow,
Each motion graceful, a fleeting show.
Their snowy wings take gentle flight,
Reflecting joy in the pale moonlight.
The cold bites soft, but they don't care,
For magic lingers in the air.
Their angels smile, their spirits gleam,
Caught in a playful winter dream.

The Canvas of Winter

The world is blank, a snowy slate,
Where children's hands create their fate.
They leap and twist, they spin and fall,
Their laughter echoes over all.
With careful sweeps, their angels grow,
Etched in fields of untouched snow.
Each form a gift, a fleeting grace,
A moment carved in winter's embrace.
They see the sky, so vast and white,
And feel their hearts take gentle flight.
For snow angels are more than play,
They're dreams unfolding where children lay.

Where Angels Dance

The snow lies deep, a sparkling bed,
Where dreams and laughter gently spread.
The children leap, their arms out wide,
Creating angels side by side.
Each sweep of snow, each kick of glee,
Reveals a wing for all to see.
They laugh and spin, their cheeks aglow,
Their hearts alive in winter's show.
Above, the stars begin to shine,
Their twinkle matching each design.
And as they play, their spirits prance,
In fields of snow where angels dance.

The Winter's Art

The snow is soft, the air is clear,
The children play without a fear.
They lie beneath the wintry skies,
And wave their arms where angels rise.
Their giggles bounce on frosty air,
As every move creates a pair—
Of wings that stretch, of halos gleam,
A child's touch on a snowy dream.
The fields transform beneath their play,
An artwork formed in cold array.
For snow angels bring love's own spark,
A masterpiece in the snowy park.

Angels in the Frost

The snow's embrace is soft and deep,
Where children dive and angels sleep.
Their arms and legs move to and fro,
Creating forms in fields of snow.
Each child becomes an artist true,
With frosty wings in every hue.
Their breath is fog, their cheeks are red,
But still they play, where angels tread.
Above, the moon begins to rise,
Its silver glow on snowy skies.
And in the frost, their laughter rings,
Where winter births her angel wings.

The Joy of Angels

The children scatter, their laughter clear,
As snowflakes fall, they leap with cheer.
They find their spots on the frozen ground,
And sweep their arms in a rhythmic sound.
Each movement shapes a snowy wing,
Their innocence a fleeting spring.
The angels bloom where none had been,
A magic born from joy within.
The frost surrounds, the sky turns blue,
Their spirits rise as angels do.
And as they run, their dreams remain,
In snow angels kissed by winter's reign.

Recipe for Christmas Cheer

Take a cup of laughter, loud and bright,
Add a dash of hope to light the night.
Mix in a spoonful of hugs so tight,
And sprinkle with stars that twinkle white.
Fold in some songs, both old and new,
Stir in warm memories shared by you.
Add a pinch of kindness, pure and sweet,
With love as the secret, to make it complete.
Bake it all in the heart's warm glow,
And watch as the Christmas spirit will grow.
Serve it with joy to those near and dear,
And savour the magic of holiday cheer.

A Holiday Blend

Start with a bowl of snowy delight,
Add a dash of family, cozy and tight.
Sprinkle in carols, soft and clear,
And fold in laughter to spread good cheer.
A pinch of wonder, a handful of peace,
Mix them together for joy's release.
Drizzle with kindness, warm and true,
And garnish with stars from midnight's view.
Let the blend simmer through Christmas night,
Creating a season both merry and bright.
Share with the world, from heart to heart,
A recipe perfect for the holiday's start.

Christmas Day Delight

Take two cups of joy, fresh and free,
Blend with a dollop of harmony.
Add a splash of giving, a sprinkle of care,
And fold in love from everywhere.
Toss in traditions, old and sweet,
And stir with the rhythm of dancing feet.
Pour in some magic, a glimmering glow,
And sprinkle with memories that softly grow.
Bake in the warmth of family's embrace,
Until every heart finds its place.
Serve with smiles and laughter's sound,
A Christmas delight that knows no bound.

Magic in the Making

Mix a heap of wonder with starlight's gleam,
Add a tablespoon of a child's dream.
Stir in compassion, smooth and warm,
And blend with comfort through any storm.
Add a pinch of snowflakes, pure and white,
And a drizzle of candles glowing bright.
Fold in memories from years gone by,
And sprinkle with wishes that touch the sky.
Let it rise with the spirit of love,
Lifted by blessings from above.
Serve it fresh with joy and grace,
A recipe that time can't erase.

A Cup of Christmas Magic

Start with a smile, as bright as the dawn,
Add the light of a tree the moment it's on.
Mix in some laughter, soft and sweet,
And a dash of goodwill for all you meet.
Fold in a handful of warm embraces,
And a sprinkle of joy from children's faces.
Add a dollop of peace, a spoonful of care,
And top it with love, beyond compare.
Let the Flavors blend through the night,
Filling hearts with warmth and light.
Serve it with hugs and gratitude true,
A Christmas recipe just for you.

Festive Flavors

Start with a base of twinkling lights,
And a layer of songs on snowy nights.
Add a pinch of dreams, both big and small,
And fold in kindness shared with all.
Mix in the glow of family near,
And the sparkle of joy in holiday cheer.
Season with stories, old and new,
And sprinkle with stars from heaven's view.
Let it rest in the heart's embrace,
A recipe made with love and grace.
Serve it warm, with smiles aglow,
For the perfect Christmas, as we all know.

Joyful Creation

Take one golden star from the sky,
Add a whisper of love as you sigh.
Blend with laughter, loud and true,
And a sprinkle of snowflakes just for you.
Mix in some carols, sung with pride,
And the warmth of friends right by your side.
Add a splash of magic, a glimmering hue,
And fold in memories, fresh as dew.
Let it simmer through the night,
Creating a Christmas, merry and bright.
Serve with hope and a dash of care,
A holiday feast for hearts to share.

The Perfect Holiday Dish

Start with a bowl of frosted delight,
Add a handful of stars to light the night.
Stir in some giggles, soft and sweet,
And mix in warmth for hands and feet.
Season with hugs from loved ones dear,
And fold in the glow of holiday cheer.
A pinch of wonder, a spoonful of grace,
Add smiles and joy in every place.
Bake with love till it's golden and bright,
A dish to savour on Christmas night.
Serve with gratitude and festive glee,
A recipe for love and harmony.

Warmth in Every Bite

Combine a spoonful of family ties,
With the twinkle of stars in winter skies.
Add a dash of giving, bold and true,
And fold in dreams both old and new.
Stir in the glow of candlelight,
And the sound of laughter through the night.
Sprinkle with hope, a measure full,
And pour in kindness till hearts are full.
Let it bake in the oven of care,
Filling the home with joy to share.
Serve it with hugs and gratitude deep,
A Christmas recipe you'll always keep.

Recipe for Holiday Magic

Take a measure of snow, so soft and white,
And mix with the glow of a firelight.
Add a dash of wonder, fresh and free,
And a sprinkle of love for family.
Blend with the sound of sleigh bells near,
And a cup of cheer for all to hear.
Fold in memories from days long past,
With hopes and dreams that forever last.
Season with smiles and hearts that care,
And bake in the warmth of love we share.
Serve it up with joy untamed,
A Christmas recipe perfectly named.

The Hidden Treasure

In a box tucked away, the years took hold,
An ornament, dusty and tinged with gold.
Forgotten amidst the newer shine,
Its beauty dimmed by the hand of time.
But one Christmas Eve, a child did see,
This hidden gem beneath the tree.
With careful hands, they lifted it high,
Its sparkle returned, as if to reply.
Hung on the bough, it seemed to glow,
A relic of love from long ago.
The forgotten treasure now takes its place,
A symbol of joy and timeless grace.

The Ornament's Song

A forgotten ornament, quiet and still,
Lay at the bottom, under the thrill.
Newer baubles had stolen its space,
Yet it held a story, a touch of grace.
One gentle hand brushed off the dust,
Revealing its shine beneath the rust.
It sang of Christmases from the past,
Of laughter shared, and love that lasts.
Placed on the tree, its beauty restored,
It twinkled as memories softly poured.
For the ornament's song, though nearly lost,
Brought back a warmth beyond all cost.

A Memory Unveiled

The ornament sat, forgotten, unseen,
Amid the sparkle of reds and greens.
Its edges dulled, its lustre gone,
A quiet relic of seasons long drawn.
But one Christmas night, a box was stirred,
And with it, the ornament's voice was heard.
It whispered of hands that once held it tight,
Of glowing trees in the soft firelight.
Hung once more on the tallest tree,
It sparkled anew for all to see.
A memory unveiled, its story true,
Of love eternal, shining through.

The Ornament's Return

Buried deep in a tangle of lights,
An ornament slept through many nights.
Forgotten beneath the glitter and cheer,
Its place untouched for year after year.
But on this Christmas, a hand reached down,
Brushing away its dusty crown.
Its faded colors began to gleam,
Reviving the glow of a long-lost dream.
Placed on a branch, it seemed to smile,
As memories danced for a little while.
The forgotten ornament found its part,
A symbol of love in every heart.

The Ornament's Secret

The ornament hid in a shadowed nook,
A silent keeper of memories it took.
Once bright with joy, now dim with dust,
Its story held in a quiet trust.
A curious child, with wonder wide,
Found the ornament where it had tried to hide.
They polished its face, they hung it high,
And watched as it twinkled beneath the sky.
The tree seemed fuller, the moment complete,
As the ornament's magic became bittersweet.
Its secret shared, its tale retold,
A Christmas treasure worth more than gold.

The Forgotten Glow

In the attic, among the forgotten and old,
Lay an ornament dulled from years of cold.
Once it had gleamed on the Christmas tree,
Now it waited in silence, patiently.
One holiday eve, a box was found,
And memories stirred with a quiet sound.
The ornament glimmered, faint but true,
As hands that loved it knew what to do.
Placed on a bough, its glow returned,
Its meaning cherished, its magic earned.
For the forgotten glow, now shining bright,
Brought love to the tree on Christmas night.

The Ornament's Revival

At the bottom of a tattered chest,
An ornament waited, long at rest.
Its colors faded, its string askew,
It had seen so much, yet no one knew.
But this year brought a curious hand,
To lift it gently, to understand.
Its story came alive with light,
Of Christmases past, so warm and bright.
It hung once more, a centrepiece,
Its presence bringing quiet peace.
The forgotten ornament now restored,
A symbol of love forever adored.

The Ornament's Tale

The ornament sat in the dimmest place,
Its beauty masked by time's embrace.
Once a treasure on Christmas trees,
Now forgotten, lost with ease.
But a child's smile and a searching eye,
Brought the ornament back to try.
They polished its sides, they held it near,
And placed it high with holiday cheer.
It sparkled anew, its tale revealed,
Of joy and warmth it long concealed.
The ornament's place was meant to be,
A shining star on the family tree.

A Treasure Reborn

The box was opened, the dust flew high,
And there the ornament seemed to lie.
Its shimmer dim, its string undone,
Its glory hidden from everyone.
But loving hands gave it new life,
Brushing away the years of strife.
Hung on the tree, it found its light,
Glowing softly in the quiet night.
A treasure reborn, a tale retold,
Of Christmas love more precious than gold.
The ornament gleamed, its place secure,
A beacon of memories forever pure.

The Ornament's Home

Hidden away in a cardboard box,
The ornament rested beneath the locks.
It once had danced in candlelight,
But now lay quiet, out of sight.
This Christmas, hands found its glow,
A treasure lost in the winter snow.
They placed it gently upon the tree,
Where it shimmered bright for all to see.
Its home restored, its magic spread,
As dreams of the past were softly fed.
The forgotten ornament claimed its part,
A piece of the season, a piece of the heart.

Whispered Promise

The snow falls soft, a quiet embrace,
Transforming the world with gentle grace.
Each flake a whisper, a word unspoken,
A vow of peace, a bond unbroken.
It wraps the earth in a pure white glow,
A reminder of hope beneath the snow.
Through winter's chill, a warmth is found,
In the promise of spring's sacred ground.
The snow's soft voice calls near and far,
"We're all connected, no matter where we are."
Its beauty reminds us to take things slow,
To cherish the promise carried by snow.

The Snow's Gentle Vow

The snow descends, a celestial stream,
A promise stitched in a winter dream.
Each flake unique, yet all the same,
A quiet hymn in nature's name.
It smooths the edges, it mends the ground,
Bringing peace where chaos is found.
A fresh new start, a world reborn,
In snow's embrace, no heart is torn.
Its vow is simple, its truth is clear:
To renew the earth, to calm our fear.
With every fall, its message grows,
A timeless promise the snow bestows.

A Blanket of Hope

The snow falls gently, a soothing hand,
A tender gift for a weary land.
Its blanket shields, its touch consoles,
A soft renewal for aching souls.
Each flake that lands is a tiny prayer,
A promise of beauty everywhere.
It tells of cycles, of endings and starts,
Of unity born in winter's heart.
For beneath the snow, the seeds will grow,
A sign of life in frost's soft glow.
The snow reminds us, both high and low,
That hope endures wherever we go.

A Silent Oath

In the still of winter, the snow takes flight,
A silent oath in the moon's soft light.
Its gentle touch, its sparkling gleam,
Carries a message, a quiet dream.
It tells of peace, of wounds that heal,
Of truths that only nature can reveal.
Each flake descends with a calming grace,
A whispered promise for every place.
The snow reminds, as it builds its cover,
That hearts can mend, that love can recover.
Its silent oath, both steady and slow,
Is hope reborn in the fall of snow.

A Promise to Renew

The snow falls soft on fields so bare,
Its frosted beauty lingers there.
It carries a promise, strong and true,
That life will thrive, that dreams renew.
Each flake is unique, a fleeting grace,
Yet together they brighten the coldest space.
They smooth the past, they cleanse the old,
Bringing warmth despite the cold.
In snow's embrace, the world takes pause,
Renewed by nature's gentle laws.
Its promise whispers in every glow,
That unity lives beneath the snow.

A Gift of Renewal

The snow arrives, a gift so pure,
Its touch a balm, its beauty sure.
It softens the earth, it stills the air,
A promise of renewal everywhere.
Its icy lace weaves hope anew,
A gift for all, for me, for you.
It tells of cycles, of time to heal,
Of gentle truths the heart can feel.
The snow reminds, with every fall,
That nature's love is meant for all.
A gift of beauty, soft and slow,
A promise wrapped in every snow.

Disclaimer for Snowflakes and Starlight: Christmas Poems for All Ages

The poems in this collection are works of creative expression, inspired by the universal themes of the Christmas season. While every effort has been made to craft content suitable for all ages, individual interpretations and sensitivities may vary.

The imagery and stories are intended to evoke a sense of wonder, nostalgia, and joy, and are not intended to reflect or promote any specific religious beliefs or practices. Readers of all backgrounds are welcome to enjoy this book as a celebration of the holiday spirit, love, and unity.

All rights to the content in this book are reserved by the author and publisher. No part of this book may be reproduced, stored in a retrieval system, or transmitted in any form by any means—electronic, mechanical, photocopying, recording, or otherwise—without prior written permission.

The creators of this book hope it brings you and your loved ones moments of peace, inspiration, and joy during the holiday season.

Happy reading and Merry Christmas!